# Finding the Birthday Cake

## Helping Children Raise Their Self-Esteem

Written and Illustrated by Elizabeth Wagele

with Judith Dome

New Horizon Press
Far Hills, NJ

## Dedication

To Chase, Savannah, Tyler, Lidia, Katya, Justin, Zoe and Amelia.

New Horizon Press
P.O. Box 669
Far Hills, NJ 07931

Wagele, Elizabeth
Finding the Birthday Cake: Helping Children Raise Their Self-Esteem
Cover Design: Norma Rahn
Interior Design: EileenTurano
Library of Congress Control Number: 2006923920

ISBN 13: 978-0-88282-277-8
ISBN 10: 0-88282-277-2

SMALL HORIZONS
A Division of New Horizon Press

2011     2010     2009     2008     2007     /     5     4     3     2     1

Printed in Hong Kong

One day as I was bopping down
the street on my way to the
grocery store, I met a
canary all dressed
up in a suit and tie.

The bird said, "How do you do.
I'm **Walter One**."

"Hey! It's unusual to meet
such a polite bird like you," I replied, taking out my notebook.
"What's up with the balloons?"

"They are for the birthday party I am giving today for my dinosaur friend," he told me. "Come inside the store with me while I buy some ice cream!"

"Very, VERY, cool," I said, as he picked the flavors.
"By the way, you look way too serious for a bird carrying funny balloons. Care to talk about what's wrong?"

"Actually, yes," said Walter One. "It might help me to talk about my problem."

"I do things right, you know. I am a good bird," he said as
we walked along. "I work hard, and I'm neat and clean."

"I follow the rules and I get other birds to follow rules," Walter One said. "For example, every night at 8 o'clock, I fly around the town to make sure the children are in the beds ON time."

"I'm a serious bird," Walter One said, "but I care about others, too."

"Oh-oh," the bird warned. "So that's my problem."

You see I decided to have a party and I made my friend a birthday cake this morning, but it isn't where I left it. I have to find it so I can have the MOST PERFECT party in the world!"

As we talked *Tina Two*, a Cocker Spaniel, came up to
us smiling a big smile
and said,

"Roses are red,
Violets are blue.
I'm going to do
Something **nice** for you."

Then she saw the worried look on her friend's face. "Tell me. What's the matter, Walter One?" she said, comfortingly, like a mommy dog. "I'll make it better…"

…and she knew just what to do to cheer him up.

Tina Two loves to take care of kids by helping them feel cozy and giving them help or advice…

"I'm helping Walter One give a party for our dinosaur friend, the Ninosaur." Then she went to help Walter decorate his nest. "You need to serve your guests good food and tell them how much you care about them," she said. "I'll help you look for the special cake you made so we can have the FRIENDLIEST party in the world!"

NEXT, a peppy frog named ***Timmy Three*** came jumping along. "I won a jumping contest yesterday!" he told me.

"That's cool, but can we talk about it later?" I asked. "Walter One is having a party and there is a cake missing and…"

"I'll find it!" Timmy Three said. "After I catch a bite to eat. Watch this!" And in no time he had caught two flies for him and two for me which he gave to me.

I couldn't eat the flies, but I praised Timmy Three for being able to catch them. As we talked, I found out a lot about Timmy Three. He's happy, likes performing, is always busy and wants to be a politician.

Timmy Three is also charming, wears nice clothes, likes to meet new people and tries hard to win.

He's eager to help when something is lost.

"I'll ask the dudes at my pond if they have seen the cake," said the green frog with the long legs. "They'll be resting between jumping contests right now."

"When we find the cake, we'll celebrate in style," he went on. "WE can have the MOST SUCCESSFUL party in the world!"

After Timmy Three hopped away, I spied
***Franny Four***, a pony, sitting quietly
on a bench.

"Do you know what is missing?" I asked the classy young lassie.

"So much is missing in my life," she said sadly. "I want to be a
dancer when I grow up and show people how I feel." And she
began to glide to and fro, shaking her tail and mane in the most
artistic way.

"Your movements are dynamite and I'm sure you'll be a wonderful dancer," I said. "But we have a more immediate problem to solve. Mr. Ninosaur's birthday cake is missing."

"How sad," she said. "I can understand how badly Walter One will feel if he can't give his friend the special cake on his birthday. When another kid suffers, I suffer, too."

"I'll help get the cake back, but I need to do it in my own way," she said. "I'll write a beautiful, fancy song and sing it all through the land. When the cake hears it, he will come running to me!"

Franny Four's friends enjoy her ability to notice and create beautiful things.

"After I find the cake, I'll dress up in my best silk and velvet clothes for the party," Franny Four told me. "We shall have the most SPECIAL party in the world!"

As I looked under every log and stone, I almost didn't see **Freddy Five**, a rabbit, sitting against a tree with his face buried in a book, reading:

*A wise old owl lived in an oak;*
*The more he saw the less he spoke;*
*The less he spoke the more he heard.*
*Why can't we all be like that wise*
*    old bird?*

When I asked if we could talk, he thought for a while. Then he said, "You're not going to bother me are you?"

"Well, there's a problem we need to solve," I said.

"In the fewest words possible, what is the problem?" he said.

"Lost cake," I answered.

Freddy Five usually likes to read alone or play quiet games with one or two friends at a time.

He watches, learns and thinks about how things work. When he feels shy, he sometimes hides or runs away.

I'm using my thinking cap for this job.

After I promised not to make any loud noises; the swift , hairy rabbit with long ears decided he'd help think about how to find the cake.

Freddy Five knows about a lot of things. "I'd like to have some long talks," he said. "We can have the MOST INTEREST-ING party in the world!"

I had the feeling something was following us.

"Who's there?" I whispered.

A handsome cat came out from behind a bush and said, "I'm *Stevie Six* and I'm trying to figure out if you're a friend or an enemy. Should I purr, smile and joke—or hiss and look scary?"

"You don't have to scare me away, dude," I said. "I don't bite."

"Pur-r-rfect!" purred Stevie Six. "Then I'll be adorable and make you laugh. Are there any high places, snakes, mice, or spiders around here?"

Stevie Six is witty, alert, and smart. Once he told me this story:

*I saw a big hairy guy with really huge feet one day.*
*He had fangs like a polar bear's.*

*His voice sounded like a hyena's*
*and his squinty eyes were way back inside his head.*

*He was licking his lips and I thought he might want to eat me*
*for his dinner.*

*I tried not to move and pretended I wasn't there.*

Stevie Six tells funny stories, jumping up and down. Sometimes he tries to calm himself by reading and writing poetry.

Sometimes he takes little chances,

but most of the time he's very cautious.

"Will you help us, furry kitty?" I asked. "The birthday cake Walter One baked is missing and the Ninosaur's party is today."

Stevie Six wouldn't join our search until Freddy Five and I promised we wouldn't let him get lost or see scary things.

Cake in bird house?

"I want the Ninosaur to know although I am jumpy around new things, I still went looking for his cake," he said. I will bring my cell phone so I can call 9-1-1 just in case, so we can have the SAFEST party in the world!"

Later we met the **Seven Cows** who had problems in school. They didn't like being told what to do and made to sit still. When they got bored, they often looked for exciting things to do, which sometimes got them into trouble.

Hee hee hee!

Here I come!

WHEE!

They dreamed about how they would celebrate after they found the cake.

Fun!

YUM!

They said they'd look for the cake everywhere because they loved to explore. Afterwards, they would tell good stories about all the places they had been and the things they'd seen.

"That way we can have the MOST FUN party in the world!"
they said.

SINCE we were now near my home, I went in to check my
e-mail and tell my tiny goldfish what was happening.

"STOP RIGHT THERE!" my fish said. "*I* WILL FIND THE
CAKE! YOU HAVE SEEN ME SWIM SO YOU KNOW HOW
STRONG I AM!" ***Amy Eight*** said in her favorite loud voice. "I'M
THE MOST CONFIDENT FISH YOU'VE EVER MET!"

*Yes! She is powerful*
*Amy Eight can*
*do figure 8's*
*in and out of her*
*fishbowl for hours*
*at a time.*

The teachers at Amy Eight's school try to get her to be quieter and more polite. But that is like asking a lion not to roar.

"I AM WHO I AM: A LEADER WHO NEVER GIVES UP. We need a hero here and I am the one for the job," Amy called out confidently.

Amy Eight loves truth and justice, looks strong, and *is* strong. She works hard and plays hard, has a mind of her own and protects kids who are weaker than she is.

This miniature superhero couldn't wait to find the cake and celebrate. "We'll eat, swim and play all day and night," she said. "We can have the MOST EXUBERANT party in the world!"

As I was reading my e-mail, I heard a soft voice say,

"I know where it is."

Slowly, a dinosaur on the wallpaper came down, laid on my bed, and said, "Do you mind if I stay a bit? I won't be any trouble."

"Er…" I said, "We are having a little problem." Then I looked closer at him. "Ninosaur! YOU MUST BE THE NINOSAUR!"

"I live here, silly," he said. "Haven't you noticed? You see, one of the Seven Cows spilled the beans and told me there was going to be a surprise for me. *'A party for little me?'* I thought. *'How sweet.'* So I took the cake and just now I was drawing this shape on top of it:

I was going to bring it to the party to surprise everyone.

"Since my friends give me such nice gifts everyday. I wanted to give them a gift, too," he said. "I've been working on the cake up there behind your wallpaper, where I keep my toothbrush and stuff."

"Do you keep the gifts they are giving you behind my wallpaper too?" I asked.

"They haven't given me things you can see," he said. "Their gifts are what they've taught me; I have learned

to want to do my best like Walter One,

to want to help others
like Tina Two,

to want to win like
Timmy Three,

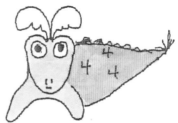

to want to be special and artistic
like Franny Four,

to want to learn a lot like
Freddy Five,

to want to figure things out and how
to be safe like Stevie Six

to want to have fun
and explore new
things like the
Seven Cows,

and to want to be
strong and confident
like Amy Eight.

"The shape I've drawn on the cake stands for the NINE KINDS
OF KIDS! It will help me teach my friends about why they are so
special—and about me."

"Tell me about yourself," I said.

"Well," the Ninosaur said, "I want us all to understand each other and I want the Earth to be a peaceful place. I'd like to help us get along and be happy so that we can have the MOST MELLOW birthday party in the world."

**Now that we had found the missing cake, we were all ready to go to the party…**

Walter One had decorated his nest for the party. Then, he explained his drawing.

"It's fun to think about what kind of kid you are," he told them, "but what I love most about each of you is that you are the ONLY ONE exactly like you!"

The Ninosaur plunked the cake in the middle of the nest and thanked Walter One for thinking of him. Everyone agreed it was the best party in the whole wide world.

# Tips for Parents and Teachers about using the Enneagram

1.  The Enneagram is an ancient system with roots in the Middle east. It is used in this book for understanding personality, encouraging self-knowledge and fostering acceptance and understanding between children.

2.  According to the Enneagram each of us has a lot of gifts, traits and learning techniques that match one of nine styles. The other eight styles are incorporated in our personalities to lesser degrees.

3.  Make working hypotheses about children's primary styles but do not tell them.

4.  Self discovery is an important aspect of learning through the Enneagram method.

5.  Don't rate one style as better than another. This can be devastating to kids whose natural styles are not the "accepted" ones.

6.  Be open to nine styles of behavior.

7.  The Enneagram shows us how to help kids of each style thrive.

8.  Learn your own Enneagram type.

# Check-list to help identify children's styles.
## —for parents, teachers and children

The child's style will probably be one of the two or three where you place the most checks.

*Check the items that apply:*

### Style ONE
### The Perfectionist

1.  tries to be fair.

2.  is orderly.

3.  tends to see things as all good or all bad.

4.  has high standards.

5.  feels guilty for making even small mistakes.

6.  is critical of self and others.

7.  works hard.

8.  tries to be good and to do things the "right" way.

9.  corrects (or wants to correct) own and others' grammar.

10. worries a lot.

11. organizes and teaches other children.

12. Speaking style may include apologizing or scolding. Might smile a lot. Some anger might show just beneath the surface.

Total ☐

# Style TWO
## The Helper

1. likes to help and give advice.

2. likes attention.

3. has easily hurt feelings.

4. tunes in easily to other people.

5. knows how to make friends.

6. tries to do well in school.

7. forms many relationships.

8. thinks of self as good.

9. is eager to please.

10. may be most comfortable with one person at a time.

11. worries about animals or other children suffering.

12. <u>Speaking style</u> may include advice-giving or using eyes for expression, dramatic language, words like "sweet."

Total ☐

# Style THREE
## The Achiever

1. is sociable.

2. is optimistic.

3. is competent.

4. works hard.

5. likes to compete and win.

6. is energetic and quick.

7. wants to get ahead. Popularity is important.

8. likes to perform for an audience.

9. will cut corners to accomplish goals.

10. is tuned in to culture. Keeps up on latest fashions.

11. is confident; may claim a skill never tried and count on being able to learn how to do it before anyone catches on.

12. Speaking style is persuasive and often to talk fast and take few pauses in order to keep the listener's attention.

Total ☐

# Style FOUR
## The Romantic

1. is creative and loves beauty.

2. is more sensitive than most kids.

3. likes to analyze and soul search.

4. tends to envy others.

5. tends to be moody and dramatic.

6. has easily hurt feelings.

7. expresses many emotions.

8. has a compassionate nature.

9. thinks of self as special.

10. tends to be melancholy, long for what is missing and suffer more than most kids.

11. has an artistic temperament - intense at times, gentle at times.

12. Speaking style may be to lament, speak dramatically and/or speak in a soft tone.

Total ☐

# Style FIVE
## The Observer

1. is quiet or shy.

2. is curious.

3. avoids conflict.

4. is sensitive to intrusion.

5. dislikes emotional displays and loud noises.

6. stays on the edge of groups, observing.

7. looks at things from many different angles.

8. is thoughtful and forms own opinions.

9. is self-sufficient and develops own interests.

10. is uninterested in social norms or goes against them.

11. has a small number of close friends and is fine being alone a lot.

12. Speaking style is to feel uneasy speaking, to speak in a gentle voice and/or to deliver a lecture. Some are very talk-ative in a nervous way.

Total ☐

## Style SIX

This is usually the most difficult number to identify. Some Sixes appear fearless (aggressive, scrappy, challenging). Some appear fearful (worried, fretful, careful). Others go back and forth from one to the other.

### The Questioner

1. wants to know what other people are thinking.
2. has a lot of energy.
3. misbehaves, is nervous or both.
4. can do excellent schoolwork.
5. sometimes blames others and/or angers easily.
6. is alert; looks for danger.
7. goes back and forth from nice to grumpy, controlling to cooperative and so on.
8. is loyal to friends, causes or groups.
9. acts strong, smart or helpless.
10. roots for the underdog (hopes the person expected to win will lose).
11. has a good sense of humor; knows what makes people laugh.
12. Speaking style is often to talk fast or to stutter (words have trouble keeping up with thoughts). Likes to debate and argue.

Total ☐

# Style SEVEN
## The Adventurer

1.  is curious.

2.  keeps busy.

3.  likes people and parties.

4.  may have many natural talents or abilities.

5.  has a sunny disposition.

6.  has a short attention span, dislikes repetition and anything slow.

7.  is friendly and sociable.

8.  will try almost anything for kicks.

9.  has several projects going at the same time, likes to have many options and plans to choose from.

10. is optimistic, quickly bounces back from anger or disappointment.

11. likes the excitement of getting into trouble (this usually applies more to males than females).

12. Speaking style is to tell adventurous stories and talk a lot. You might hear repeated requests when wanting something.

Total ☐

## Style EIGHT
## The Asserter

1. is independent and competitive.

2. loves truth and justice.

3. shows anger freely, sometimes getting into trouble for it.

4. is enthusiastic.

5. is confident, takes charge, makes up rules for others to follow.

6. is a natural leader.

7. is powerful so people know when this child is around.

8. has more energy than most kids—may want to play when others are tired.

9. is often regarded by others as someone to fear, which isn't always true.

10. is protective of those unable to defend themselves.

11. doesn't want to appear weak and only a few trusted people are allowed to see soft side.

12. Speaking style includes a strong, confident voice. Eights are more likely than most to use profanity.

Total ☐

## Style NINE
## The Peacemaker

1. tries to blend in and not rock the boat.

2. has easily hurt feelings.

3. is usually sweet and generous.

4. avoids conflicts and tries to settle them.

5. watches a lot of TV if allowed and likes to collect things.

6. has rare but explosive outbursts of anger.

7. becomes stubborn, especially when pushed.

8. likes to be comfortable; for example, relaxing in the sun.

9. is optimistic; sees the world through rose-colored glasses.

10. has trouble making decisions. Procrastinates.

11. can see things from other people's viewpoints. Is fair.

12. Speaking style is to talk rather slowly and to tell long stories. May ramble or take a long time to say goodbye, for example.

Total ☐

1 2 3 4 5 6 7 8 9